The House of Shadows

Karen Dolby

Adapted by Katie Daynes

Illustrated by
Adrienne Kern

Reading Consultant: Alison Kelly
University of Surrey Roehampton

Contents

Chapter 1

Moving house

Shirts and shoes went flying as Ned and Kit Light rushed around packing their things. Tomorrow, they were moving house and there was still so much to do.

Kit heard the letterbox clink and raced to the door. On the doormat lay an envelope with an exotic stamp, addressed to the Light family. Ripping it open, this is what she saw:

Dear Mr. and Mrs. Light,

We request your presence in Mythika, to deal with an important family matter and to claim what is rightfully yours. Enclosed are two plane tickets.

Yours urgently,

Marcus Woolittle

Marcus Doolittle, Lawyer

SKY HIGH AIRLINES INC.

Light / Mr. Thomas
Light / Mrs. Connie

From
Grand Central Airport

To
Mythika

Date
September 10th
Time
3:30pm

OPEN RETURN

Kit passed the letter to her parents, then sped upstairs to tell her brother Ned.

Sounds like we'll have to move house by ourselves.

While they fly off to sunny Mythika!

Mr. and Mrs. Light were very confused. They had no idea why they were needed in Mythika.

"We'd better go," decided Mr. Light. "It sounds important..."

In the morning, Mr. and Mrs. Light had just enough time to drop Kit and Ned at the new house, before driving on to the airport.

We'll be fine!

Mrs. Daly will drop in to check you're OK.

Hallows Grange, at One Spectral Lane in Hallows-on-the-Hill, looked gloomy, unloved and far from new.

"At least we're only renting," thought Kit, shivering.

With all their boxes unpacked,
Ned, Kit and Scruff the dog found
themselves alone. From nowhere,
an old man appeared.

"So you're moving into the
house of shadows," he said.
"You might be the ones
they're looking for." And, in
a swirl of mist, he was gone.

"How weird!" said Ned.
"Never mind, let's explore."

7

Chapter 2

Shadows and mist

Inside, the house was dark and
damp. A stale smell clung to the
old-fashioned furniture and dusty
portraits hung on every wall. Kit
and Ned flung open the windows.

"I wonder who lived here before," whispered Kit. Up a creaking staircase she found a snug attic bedroom. "I'll sleep here," she decided excitedly.

Without warning, a radio on the bed crackled into life.

"Ahhh!" screamed Kit fleeing downstairs and bumping into Scruff, who was busy growling... at nothing.

Kit rushed to the sitting room, where Ned had lit a roaring fire. After beans on toast and chocolate, they felt much better...

...until an icy gust made them both shudder. "Where's that funny white mist coming from?" asked Ned.

"And why are the shadows moving?" added Kit.

The mist swirled thicker and thicker, then disappeared. Kit and Ned looked around in amazement. Light streamed in through the window and everything seemed newer and brighter.

"What's happening?" cried Kit. "Where are we?"

"I don't know," said Ned. "But look outside. It's like a movie!"

The street bustled with ducks, carts and people in old-fashioned clothes. Kit and Ned crept outside.

"Wow!" cried Ned. "Look at our house – it's huge!"

Sure enough, their home was now just a small wing of a much larger stone building. As they watched, the main door swung open and a tall, sinister man stepped out, dragging a pale-faced boy.

The man stood impatiently as the boy's mother and sister said a tearful farewell.

"Time to go," said the man gruffly, pulling the boy into a carriage and slamming the door. They rumbled off down a cobbled street.

As Ned and Kit watched the sad scene, a chilling mist appeared, swallowing everyone and everything.

13

Chapter 3

Nightmares

Seconds later, Ned and Kit found themselves back by the fire.

"What's going on?" asked Kit.

"No idea," said Ned, still shaking, "but I'm not staying down here!"

They went up to bed and tried to sleep. Ned was nodding off, when something made him sit up with a jolt. Had someone said his name?

It was dark outside but a big, ornate mirror gleamed bright as day. He rubbed his eyes and looked at the reflection. It showed his room as it must have been centuries ago.

A shiver went down Ned's spine as he realized his own reflection

was missing. He stared harder and the pale-faced boy from the carriage stared back.

Meanwhile, Kit was dreaming of ice cream in Mythika...

...when angry voices woke her.

She could just make out two
ghostly faces. It was that horrible
man – Mr. Hubble – and the sister
of the poor boy he'd taken away.

As the voices grew louder, the
figures became more real and Kit's
room seemed to change. The sister
fled through a door that had
appeared in the wall and the man
chased after her.

"I must help,"
thought Kit, trying
the door herself.

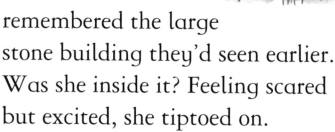

It opened onto
an endless
corridor. Kit
remembered the large
stone building they'd seen earlier.
Was she inside it? Feeling scared
but excited, she tiptoed on.

She glanced across at a mirror
and saw nothing.

"It's as if I'm not
really here," she
whispered
nervously.
"Maybe I'm a
ghost in this
house..."

Kit was about to turn back when she heard a girl crying. "The sister needs me," she decided. Feeling braver, she raced on through doors and deserted rooms.

Finally, she entered a leafy greenhouse and stopped dead. There stood the grim figure of Mr. Hubble. He slowly turned to face her and everything went dark.

Chapter 4

Detective work

It was already mid-morning when Ned woke up. He puzzled over his strange dream and looked up at the mirror. A word had been scrawled in the dust on the glass.

The door handle turned and Ned let out a scream.

"It's only me," said Kit. "You'll never guess what's happened…"

As they exchanged their spooky stories, they made toast and hot chocolate, before wandering out into the sunny garden.

"We can't both have been dreaming," said Kit between slurps.

"But what were we seeing?" said Ned. "Shadows from the past?"

"I'm not sure," replied Kit, "but I want to find out more about the house. Let's see if someone in town knows something."

It was market day, so Hallows-on-the-Hill was busier than usual.

First, Kit and Ned went into a mini supermarket.

"We've just moved into Hallows Grange," Ned said cheerfully, as he paid for some Mango Melts.

There was a shocked gasp. Worried customers scuttled away and the shopkeeper hastily announced that he was closed.

"He wasn't very friendly!" said Kit, as they wandered off. "Let's see if we have more luck in this café."

Perched on stools, they asked instead if anyone knew the old man with a walking stick. But the café staff just had more questions.

The two young detectives headed home none the wiser.

"Ned? Kit?" called a soft voice. "Were you looking for me?"

They recognized the old man – but how did he know their names?

"I'm Amos Goodfellow," he continued. "I believe you've seen the house of shadows."

They nodded and listened silently to Mr. Goodfellow, as an amazing story unfolded.

"Long ago, this house was owned by the Golightly family. They were kind landowners who held parties for everyone in the town."

"But everything changed when cruel Mr. Hubble took over under mysterious circumstances..."

"Both he and the house were haunted by shadows. One day, there was a terrible fire. Only your wing of the house survived. But at night, the shadows still come."

Kit wanted to ask more about the shadows, but Amos had gone.

Chapter 5

The house's secrets

Kit and Ned walked home, more confused than ever. As they reached the house, a curtain twitched.

"Stop right there!" Kit yelled at a fleeting shadow. "I'm going to get to the bottom of this."

Ned watched her run off. "She's braver than me!" he thought. Creeping into the kitchen, he found Kit, red with embarrassment, and a friendly woman serving up a delicious-smelling soup.

"I'm Tilda Daly," she said, before Ned could ask. "Your parents asked me to pop in while they're away."

Do you know anything about the people who lived here?

I don't, dear. But there are boxes full of papers in the attic.

After Mrs. Daly had gone, Kit and Ned clambered up to the attic. "Why didn't we think of looking up here before?" said Ned.

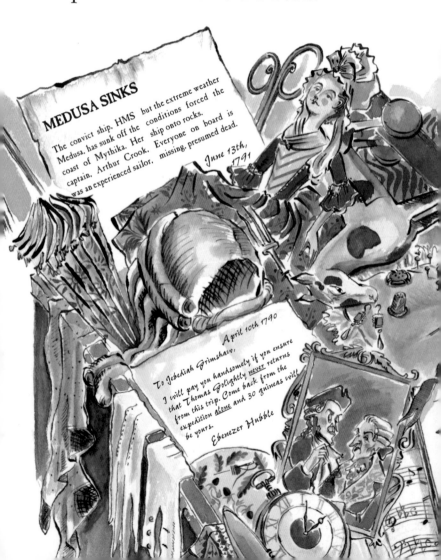

MEDUSA SINKS

The convict ship, HMS Medusa, has sunk off the coast of Mythika. Her captain, Arthur Crook, was an experienced sailor, but the extreme weather conditions forced the ship onto rocks. Everyone on board is missing, presumed dead.

June 13th, 1791

April 10th 1790

To Jebediah Grimshaw,

I will pay you handsomely if you ensure that Thomas Golightly *never* returns from this trip. Come back from the expedition *alone* and 30 guineas will be yours.

Ebenezer Hubble

Kit found an old chest, with its heavy lid already open. "It's as if someone wants us to see inside!" she said. "Let's see if these papers explain what's going on."

The Last Will & Testament of Lord Thomas Golightly of All Hallows

I leave Ebenezer Hubble in charge of my estate. When my son, Edward, reaches the age of 21, he will inherit everything. My wife Constanza and daughter Catharine, may live on at Hallows Grange. Ebenezer will manage their incomes.

T. Golightly

Ned and Kit started reading, but it was tricky piecing together the past. Then the mists began swirling again. The house was about to reveal more shadows…

The brother and sister were in the garden, speaking in hushed voices. Kit and Ned listened eagerly.

"Catherine, I can't believe our luck," said the boy, quietly. "The key to Father's safe was just lying on the dining room table! Now I can get my money and you can use it to escape."

"Oh Edward, thank you," replied Catherine. "I just wish you would come too."

"No, I must stay with Mother," said Edward. "We can't let Hubble drive us all from our home."

33

Edward headed into the house. "Let's follow him!" whispered Kit. Key in hand, Edward entered a study and unlocked a secret safe in the wall. As he counted his father's coins, Ned caught sight of Hubble, hiding behind a chair.

Mist shrouded the room, before revealing another scene. Hubble was accusing Edward of theft.

"It was a trap!" yelled Ned, but only Kit could hear him.

The mist swirled up again, taking them back to the study.

This time, sneaky Hubble was removing a green-edged document from a drawer and replacing it with one from inside his coat.

Finally, the mist brought Ned and Kit back to their own time. They were in the attic again and an old newspaper cutting lay at their feet. They began to read.

Lord's son found guilty of theft

Edward Golightly, son of the late Lord Thomas Golightly of All Hallows, stood trial for theft today. He was accused of stealing gold coins from his father's cousin, Ebenezer Hubble, who is now in charge of the All Hallows estate. Edward's sister, Catherine, was seen weeping in the courtroom.

At yesterday's trial Hubble was quoted as saying, "It saddens me to bring the boy to trial – he is my beloved cousin's son. But he has disgraced the family's reputation and shamed his father's name. Justice must be done, however painful."

Edward Golightly in the dock.

Judge Hubert Stern summed up by saying, "Mr. Hubble's evidence against the boy leaves me no alternative but to sentence him to seven years in the colonies."

Many were shocked by the harsh punishment. Edward Golightly will sail on the Medusa convict ship, which leaves on March 30th.

Friday, February 24th 1791

"The Medusa!" gasped Kit, remembering a newspaper article in the chest. "It sank, so poor Edward must have drowned…"

37

A gust of air blew another piece of paper onto Ned's lap.

"It's the document Hubble took from the drawer," said Ned.

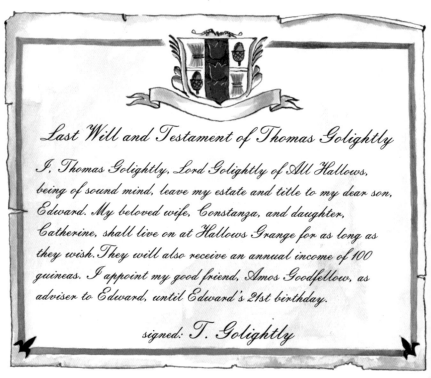

Last Will and Testament of Thomas Golightly

I, Thomas Golightly, Lord Golightly of All Hallows, being of sound mind, leave my estate and title to my dear son, Edward. My beloved wife, Constanza, and daughter, Catherine, shall live on at Hallows Grange for as long as they wish. They will also receive an annual income of 100 guineas. I appoint my good friend, Amos Goodfellow, as adviser to Edward, until Edward's 21st birthday.

signed: T. Golightly

"If this is Lord Golightly's real will," whispered Kit, "the one in the chest must be a fake!"

Chapter 6

The truth

The shadows hadn't finished telling their story. More mist came and went, unveiling a lawyer speaking after Lord Golightly's death. He was reading from the fake will.

Ebenezer Hubble is now in charge of Thomas Golightly's estate.

"But how did Lord Golightly die?" whispered Ned. The next scene told him the answer.

Grimshaw says Thomas was attacked by wild beasts and died!

Grimshaw did a good job. It was worth paying him all that money!

"There was a letter to Grimshaw in that old chest," said Kit. "Did Hubble really pay him to get rid of Lord Golightly? That's terrible!"

A now familiar swirling sensation took Kit and Ned back to the study, where Hubble sat at the desk.

"This is all too confusing," hissed Ned. His ghostly presence made Hubble wince.

"I'm haunted by echoes," Hubble muttered, as he scribbled notes in a leather-bound book.

"It's his diary!" whispered Kit. She peered closer to read it.

I feel someone's watching me...

December 1st 1791

Through my trickery, Edward is safely out of the way. Hallows Grange is mine! And yet at night, when all is quiet, I miss Thomas. He was my cousin and childhood friend after all. But when he planned that ridiculous jungle trip, I saw my chance. I hired Grimshaw as a fake guide and arranged for Thomas to get eaten by animals. Replacing his will was easy!

But now, when the shadows gather, I am afraid. Is it guilt that stops me destroying the real will?

Ah well, what's done is done. I just wish my son Gervase would play his part. He needs to impress Catherine and marry her. Then the Hallows' title and inheritance will be ours!

Suddenly, Hubble jumped to his feet, sending Kit and Ned back into the shadows.

"My son, Gervase, will marry Catherine, whether she likes it or not!" he exclaimed.

Then the estate will belong to the Hubbles forever!

There was a knock at the door
and a servant came in.

Hubble tore open the letter and
clasped his head in despair. "No
one must ever know!" he screamed.

Ned grabbed the letter as it floated to the ground. Eagerly, he and Kit read it.

Mythika
September 5th, 1791

Dear Madam,

I was Midshipman on HMS Medusa. I wish you to know that myself and your son, Edward, survived when the ship capsized. We are both very weak and Edward has lost his memory. He will need his family's help to get him home safely.

Your obedient servant,

Samuel Tar

"It's from Mythika!" cried Kit. Then they noticed Hubble staring at them – or rather, at the letter. He couldn't see Ned's hand and thought the letter was floating!

Help!

Chapter 7

Finding the lake

Everything blurred and grew misty. When it cleared, Kit and Ned were back in their own time and downstairs.

"I'm exhausted!" cried Kit. "Why are we being shown all this?"

With a sudden crackle, the TV came on. Three ghostly figures appeared on the screen – Hubble, his son Gervase and Amos.

Poor Catherine drowned in the lake last night.

This is all your fault, Gervase.

A shrill ringing noise made Kit and Ned jump. But it was only their mother phoning from Mythika.

The line was really bad. All Kit could make out was something about their great grandfather changing his name from Golightly to Light.

"Ned!" cried Kit. "We're related to the Golightlys!"

"Then we must help Edward and Catherine," Ned replied. "Wait a minute – those are *our* real names!"

They looked around, anxious for the next clue, but the house was disappointingly normal. Night came and still there was no mist. Kit and Ned waited for hours, not wanting to sleep.

We don't know how Catherine drowned...

Maybe we've seen everything now.

49

Finally, the mists gathered, taking Ned and Kit back to shadow time.

"Quick! To the lake," cried Ned, finding himself outside. Lashed by rain and struggling against the wind, they darted through trees... and found they weren't alone. Hubble was shaking Gervase in a panic.

Amos was waiting in the distance.

Catherine should be here soon.

And there was Catherine, rushing through the trees, dressed as a boy and carrying some clothes.

When Hubble finds my clothes, he'll think I've drowned!

"She's heading for the lake,"
said Kit.

"But Hubble's chasing after her,"
Ned added. "Quick!"

They reached the lakeside and
stared in horror. Catherine was
struggling with Hubble on a little
jetty, above the murky water.

"He'll push her in," said Kit.
"Then she'll drown for real!"

"We must do something," said
Ned, desperately.

Spotting Catherine's cloak, he
held it up high and crept onto
the jetty.

Beside him, Kit waved a wooden
oar from a little boat. All Hubble
and Catherine could see were a
billowing cloak and a haunted oar.

"Agghhh!" cried Hubble, as Ned flung the cloak over his head. Catherine saw her chance and fled through the trees.

"Let's make him think she's drowned," said Kit. While Hubble struggled with the cloak, Kit overturned the wooden boat and Ned chucked Catherine's hat into the lake.

Chapter 8

Home sweet home

Whirling leaves masked the scene, then all was calm. It was morning and Kit and Ned were back in their own time.

"Look," called Kit, "Amos is in our garden!"

They rushed outside to greet the old man, who seemed to know all about their adventures.

"Time has passed," he whispered. "Hubble is haunted by guilt. His end is near. On the day he dies, you must tell everyone the truth."

"When did he die?" asked Ned, but once again Amos had vanished.

"We'll have to find out for ourselves," sighed Kit.

"Umm... there's a graveyard near here," said Ned. "If we can find his gravestone, we'll know the date."

In the evening sun, the graveyard looked very peaceful.

Alone in a gloomy corner stood Hubble's gravestone.

"Look at the date," whispered Kit. "It's today!"

Ebenezer Hubble
Died 12th September
1792

Darkness was falling as Kit and Ned reached home. It wasn't long before the mist arrived and they were taken back to the house of shadows.

"I hear voices," cried Kit. "Let's see where they're coming from."

They followed the voices into a room where Hubble lay dying.

People crowded around the
bedside, to hear Hubble's will.

"To his son, Gervase, he leaves
this estate," announced the lawyer.

"Hubble stole this house!" cried
Ned, but only Kit heard. What
were they to do?

Just then, the door opened and
Amos walked in. He stared at Kit
and Ned, then looked at the
bookshelf. Kit followed his gaze
and saw... Hubble's diary.

The diary contained proof of his crimes. Kit snatched it from the shelf, sending other books flying. As she carried it over to the lawyer, everyone gasped – except Hubble, who quaked beneath his blanket.

"It appears I have something else to read," said the lawyer, in surprise. He began to read aloud from the diary.

"By his own hand, Mr. Hubble has admitted his guilt," declared the lawyer, at last. "This house was never lawfully his, so his son can never inherit it."

Kit and Ned wanted to hear more, but they were swirled into the garden. Time had moved on and Catherine and Edward were both back, looking very happy.

Finally, the story was over. Kit and Ned had solved an ancient crime, Edward had been rescued from Mythika, the house belonged to the Golightlys again and the terrible fire had never happened.

Mist swirled around Kit and Ned for the last time, bringing them back to the present. To their delight, their house was now a grand mansion, inherited from their ancestors.

Series editor: Lesley Sims
Cover design: Russell Punter

First published in 2004 by Usborne Publishing Ltd., Usborne House,
83-85 Saffron Hill, London EC1N 8RT, England. www.usborne.com
Copyright © 2004 Usborne Publishing Ltd.